THOMAS AND THE BAD DOG

CHRISTOPHER AWDRY
ILLUSTRATED BY KEN STOTT

HEINEMANN · LONDON

Thomas was waiting at the station. His driver was on the platform reading the newspaper.
"There's a stray dog chasing sheep in the valley," the driver said.

"Dogs don't bother me," said Thomas. "If I see him I'll just blow steam at him. He'll soon go away then."
The signal arm dropped and Thomas's driver climbed into the cab. The whistle blew and they set off down the line.

The Fat Controller looked at his watch.
"Right on time," he said to himself. "What a Really
Useful Engine Thomas is."

As Thomas approached the tunnel, he said "Hello" to
James who was coming through on the other line.

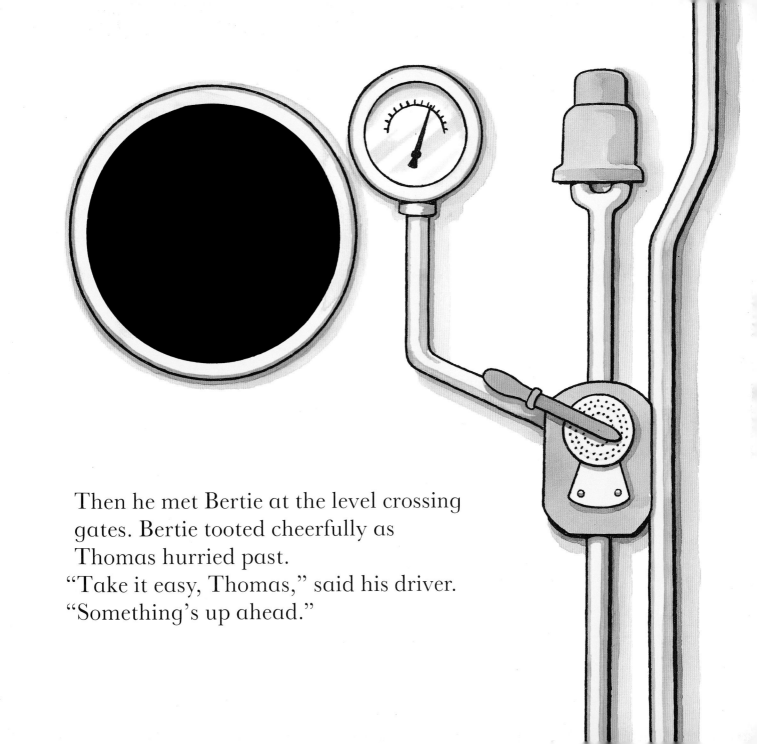

Then he met Bertie at the level crossing
gates. Bertie tooted cheerfully as
Thomas hurried past.
"Take it easy, Thomas," said his driver.
"Something's up ahead."

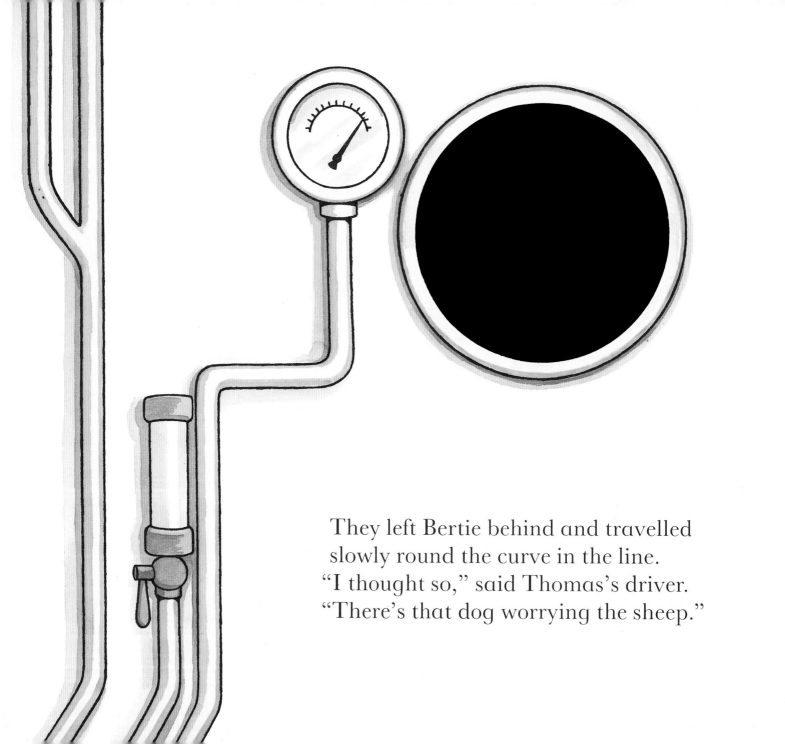

They left Bertie behind and travelled
slowly round the curve in the line.
"I thought so," said Thomas's driver.
"There's that dog worrying the sheep."

Suddenly Thomas saw the hedge shake and a sheep jumped out onto the line. It was followed by another and another and another.

"Whoa, Thomas," said his driver, just as a dog chased the sheep across the line.

Now there were sheep everywhere. Thomas stopped
with a loud "Whoosh!"
The dog looked scared and ran away at once,
but the sheep huddled together on the railway line.

Soon a worried-looking farmer appeared. The sheep were badly frightened and it took the farmer a long time to round them up. This made Thomas very late and when he tried to start he found he couldn't.

"I'm sorry I've held you up," said the farmer.
"Don't worry. We know it's not your fault," Thomas's driver replied.

The guard went down to warn the signalman that Thomas was blocking the line.

At last Thomas was mended.
"Come on, we're late. Come on, we're late," he puffed.
"Don't go so fast. Don't go so fast," called Annie and Clarabel. But Thomas was in such a hurry he didn't even see Percy on the other line.

"You're in a hurry, Thomas," Percy called. But Thomas had already flashed past and was stopping at the next station. The passengers got out and Thomas waited impatiently for the guard to blow his whistle and wave his green flag.

But there was no whistle and no green flag.
"Where is the guard?" asked Thomas.
"We tried to tell you. We left him behind,"
said Annie and Clarabel.

Soon the guard came
running up the line.

"Wait for me, Thomas," called the guard.
"Sorry we went without you," said Thomas.
"What a bad journey we've had. Now we're *really* late."
"Better late than never, Thomas," said his driver.

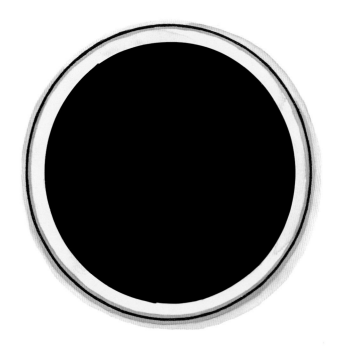

He patted Thomas's boiler.
"And you did a grand job scaring that dog away with
your whooshing," he said. "He won't be worrying the
sheep any more. The Fat Controller has just phoned to
say how pleased he is with you."

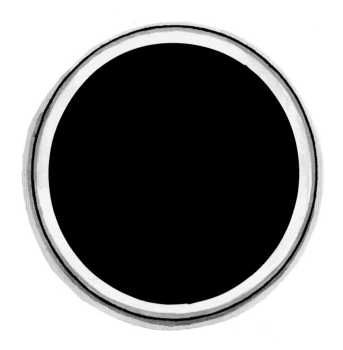

This made Thomas so happy he forgot
all about being late.
"Well done, Thomas."

William Heinemann Ltd
Michelin House
81 Fulham Road
London SW3 6RB

LONDON MELBOURNE AUCKLAND

First published in 1990
Copyright © William Heinemann 1990

ISBN 0 434 97615 6

Produced by Mandarin
Printed and bound in Hong Kong